love in the time
of metal and flesh

love in the time of metal and flesh

of metal and flesh

Jay Lake

PRIME BOOKS

LOVE IN THE TIME
OF METAL AND FLESH

Interior design and typesetting by Garry Nurrish.

Prime Books
www.prime-books.com

ISBN: 978-1-60701-340-2

Id: Precursor

I am become machine. Tiny springs click broken-backed and slack-spiraled deep within my lungs as my bellows-breath rattles in the iron cage of my ribs. My blood is the sour oil of regret. My bile is the musty taste of lost wisdom and found sorrow. When I try to move my fingers, they clack with the rust of years and the straining of gears, my touch reaching for something which I cannot quite see.

There is nothing to see. Oily dark marks the black I can reach with what remains to me. This transformation, it has become my life, my art, myself. This transformation has become me.

α: Love in the Time of Metal

Distant doctors chatter and chaffer, their words a susurrus caressing his ears as the ocean caresses the shore. Machines whisper as well, their quiet clicking and gentle beeping a womb for the dying, ushering the man who was toward the soul who will be. Or won't.

There is honest confusion and dishonest amusement on that subject. To be possessed of a soul implies an obligation towards ethics, morality, behavior to which one can live up in the face of ultimate judgment. He wonders—his mind floating free on an ocean of pharmaceuticals, dancing freely within the chemical pathways of his neurophysiology—

wonders on the link between cause and action, between thought and deed, between the weak and palsied vibrato of the human heart and whatever might pass for the vessel of the human body.

"Love is a fountain," he says. No words pass the space where his lips once were.

The machine-beeps change tone, acquiring a plaintive tone in pursuit of his eventual health and healing. Doctor voices change.

"Love," he says again, "is a *fountain*. Can you hear me?"

Noise degrades to fractured fractal silence, punctuated by the rubber screech of nurses' shoes and the whispers of the dying.

Has time passed, he wonders?

"Can you hear me?"

The silence bounces, echoing down metal shafts and through long hallways of cartilage to impinge on the slow syrup of his thoughts.

"Can you hear me? I'm talking about love."

"Love," says a woman with her final breath.

"Is," cries an infant in a distant ward.

"The most human," coughs a tubercular with the last bloody bit of his lungs.

"Mistake of all," the machines echoes.

i: Love in the Time of Flesh

Markus spent years planning the first cut. Danni had been helpful, bringing him books, taking him to torture room parties. Sometimes even more special field trips.

One day she came by his apartment. Markus was carving Celtic knots into the skin side of a slab of pork. Practicing. It was his day off from the bookstore job, when he could think even less than usual.

"Hey, hon," Danni said, slipping through the door and walking across the room to plant a kiss on his forehead. She clanked when she walked, as she always did—six metal bars set into the inside of each thigh. Not that she had a lot of extra flesh for such work, but somehow Danni managed. "Got a surprise for you."

"Mmm . . . " Markus was trying to work out how to cut a loop and keep the center skin in place. "How's things?"

"Oh, you know. Metal. Surprise, Markus. You listening?"

He looked up. Her hair was orange this month, about the color of shrimp on a low-end sushi bar, and she'd been inking her face with laundry marker camouflage patterns in sympathy with the current war. "Listening now," he said, though he kept the scalpel steady in his hand.

"Daddy Nekko set you up with something special."

Markus didn't like Daddy Nekko. Daddy Nekko had far too much of a hold on Danni's time and imagination for his comfort—he'd thought that before they'd started sleeping together, and he'd keep thinking that long after she was done with him. Daddy Nekko had put the bars into Danni's thighs. The damned things hurt Markus' temples every time he went down on her.

"What kind of special?" he asked, his voice slow and low.

"Your kind of special, hon." She kissed him again, took the scalpel away, and curled up on his lap, sitting half on his pork skin.

Danni drove, her little gold Honda Civic plastered with Goth girl stickers—Born to Cry, It's All About the Pain: The Metal's Just a Souvenir, My Other Girlfriend Lives in a Box. Markus hated folding himself in and out of the car. He was several inches too tall not to bang something on the body every God damned time.

Danni only laughed, same as she ever did. "You're a big lunk who deserves to go thunk."

"Fuck you," he said amiably.

"Later."

Then they were off through the intestinal avenues of San Francisco, Danni throwing the gear shift around with a mad abandon which promised to make some mechanic's house payment soon. Markus sank into his seat, covered with some weird Hawaiian shirt fabric, and closed his eyes, letting the swaying and banging of the little car take him wherever Danni wanted to go.

When she slammed to a halt, he opened his eyes and looked around. They hadn't crossed a bridge or headed along a highway, so they had to be somewhere in San Francisco proper. Down by Army Street maybe? Chavez, whatever it was now. The Civic idled along on a quiet avenue of crumbling warehouses, two- and three-storey facades from a time when even the utilitarian was a subject of pride. Art deco capitals topped fake columns now eroded to lines on plaster, while pigeons nested among the iron ruins of once-proud signs long gone to glass powder and stubbed, rusted wires.

The only other vehicle in sight was an aging eighteen-wheeler, cab the color of a junkyard, trailer covered with peeling, leprous paint in the remains of what had once been a hippie mural celebrating organic produce, or perhaps the victory of the People's Vegetable Army. The truck was backed up the loading dock of one of the warehouses, a tarp dropped down to cover whatever was being transferred.

"You owe Daddy Nekko," she said quietly.

For what? Markus wanted to say, but he knew better than to ever argue with Danni. Especially not when she was like this. Previous sudden excursions had resulted rather memorably in a group sex session with a lesbian biker gang

9

consisting of an astonishingly high percentage of East Asian midgets, a trip to a 'shroom farm in Mendocino where he'd gotten higher than he'd believed possible, and a night in an abandoned jail talking to a man who believed he was Jesus and had performed some convincing sleight-of-hand with cheap red wine.

In short, Danni had conditioned Markus to expect anything, despite his native cynicism.

"Wait 'til they're done," she whispered. She then dug into her minimal cleavage for a spliff about the size of a fat-point sharpie which she proceeded to light off and share with Markus.

He descended into a pleasant haze of green tobacco and watched while the leprous trailer rocked as if giants were having sex within.

Sail Selvage: A Portrait

Selvage, Sail; Senior, 1979

Drama club, home economics club, recreational band

"She can slice and dice with the best of 'em, dude."

—Spanky Fuentes

"Best dancer in the senior class."

—Mindy Carstairs

The photo is of a beautiful girl, brunette hair falling over one side of her face in the classic yearbook twist. Her eyes are half-

lidded, with a sultry look that any thirty-year-old chicken hawk knows all too well. She's thin, rail-thin, the kind of girl a man could almost put both hands around. There's a lot of miss-you-babes written in her yearbook, notes from boys who had it good with her and are wondering if the college girls will be any better than a home girl with spreading legs and a smile nicer than Mom's.

Superego: Judgment

Oh, God, what have I done? This isn't what I meant.

I can barely breathe. When they ask me to blink, it doesn't quite work. I can see Dr. Thompson's files, while he talks to that nurse with the garlic breath. There is a scan clipped to the top. MRI or something. I don't know, but it is . . . like seeing a demon of me. What the hell are they scanning me with? I don't remember any tests that would make me look like . . . that.

My eyes are drawn, and turn away at once. Like a kid playing with magnets that spring together or apart again depending on the poles. It is me, part of me, inside me, a piece of me.

And I cannot look at it.

I feel sick, sick as I had the first time I'd cut away a part of my body. My toe. Pinkie. Small enough to be lopped with a pair of bull dykes with blue electrical tape on the handle and an old Sears price tag still clinging to one red plastic-sheathed handle. It fell away, no bigger than the nub of a peanut, and my blood poured like an orgasm from my foot, me laughing and giggling into the tub until I was faint with heat from the shower steam and blood loss and wrapped duct tape around my foot, the entire roll until it was a big silver-gray ball, and I couldn't walk for days and God damn me, I cannot look at that scan the color of the dark side of duct tape, black as old blood, my face shriveled as the toe which yet sits in a sugar bowl on my desk, my eyes starting from inside, rippled spread of skull like the ocean's whipped waves frozen to dark plastic and something that might have crept from inside the freshest of wounds, a guilty grin upon its face.

My face.

There is a guilty grin upon my face.

Oh, God, what I have done?

I love her.

Loved.

Love.

It is all my doing.

Liver and Lights

Surging dark surf, roiling through channels like Noah's flood sent down a thousand miles of concrete ductwork. All the world's filth passes here, the East River of the human body, the place where everything comes to die, or migrates to in the time after death, ever seeking repatriation with the great unknown.

Markus sails the standing wave of heme, wallowing in his own oxygenation, dodging killer t-cells and the mighty whites that sound and thrash amid the depths of the vessels and vesicles which writhe within him. He is not sure if this is a voyage of the mind or a voyage of the body. While he has handled several livers in his life, he is fairly certain that he has never seen his own, not from the inside.

A voice echoes in his head, long ago preaching from a high lectern, a distant, fearsome man with a slap-leather Bible in one hand and a metal belt-end in the other. "And so the Bible does tell us, in the book of Lamentations: Mine eyes do fail with tears, my bowels are troubled, my liver is poured upon the earth, for the destruction of the daughter of my people!"

My liver is poured upon the earth, Markus thinks, *and me with it.* Then he is within, passing ever smaller into the network of channels and canales which interpenetrate the lobes more tightly than ever any two lovers found a way to be one.

"What?" grumbles the liver. The voice is a rumbling mix of thunder and fear, toxic echoes in the undertones of a busy someone—something?—turning reluctant attention to a necessary if regrettable gadfly.

"I'm sorry," Markus says. He doesn't mean it, and his liver knows. The mind can lie to itself, but not to the body.

There is a whiff, sewers and hospitals mixed together in an unholy duo of sepsis. The liver does protest.

"So . . . ?" The voice now like gravel sliding down a cliff, pushing boulders onto a stalled school bus.

"I need to know . . ." He cannot remember now what it is he means to ask. "I need to know why . . . how . . . what . . . "

"Why?" The liver is ponderous, nearly angry now, enfolding him like the wrath of Mother. "Why? Why have you visited the filth and poisons of the world upon me? Why have you driven yourself past breaking me? Why have you swallowed so much cum, so much spew, so much woman sweat?"

"No." Markus struggles for clarity. Distant machines whicker, complaining of ill health, stress, the onset of Cheyne-Stokes respiration and ketone breath, and other premortem breakdowns. "I want something else," Markus says.

Even the angry liver can hear the external threats. It squeezes him tight, purpling meat enfolding him until the breath leaves his lungs and his heart skips beats, economizing the last jolts of energy in the face of this most bizarre autoimmune suicide. "What do you want?"

He is weeping now, fear and regret mixed in a stone

14

soup of the soul. "Love is a fountain. What became of my love? What became of my love?"

"Ah . . ." The liver releases him to the flow of his blood, the pounding of his pulse. Markus is swept away, borne beyond consciousness and sense into some other territory that means less and less with each washing beat, cleansed of his toxins and baptized in bile, a new man, whole—in a sense—made into something else, his own fears temporarily taken up in the twinned lobes of the great filter of his body.

β: *Love in the Time of Metal*

He has become aware of linoleum. It is a nineteenth-century miracle of materials science borne forth into the twenty-first century on a wave of legacy flooring and ruptured maintenance budgets. There is linoleum beneath him, its ancient linseed oil surging slowly upward through layers of vinyl and hypoallergenic underlayment.

His veins are linoleum, too, or possibly Teflon. He is unsure now. There had been a project once, replacing some of his venous routing with external tubing. Surgical staples clung to his body, crisscrossed with tape in pleasing colors and patterns, bearing the dark and viscous blood home to the heart. The engineering of the human circulatory system had confounded him, then, but later, there had been more cleverness.

Now he is aware of linoleum, even as he sinks further

and faster into the floor. He is spreading thin, his blood spilling out to a barely visible slick, the cells dissolving into tiny, purposeless machines that will wander the cracks and interstices of the hospital forever, each carrying a whispered fragment of his soul until he is attenuated into the very fabric of the ancient building and each brick whispers and whimpers his name.

Her name.

His lost, lovely, luscious love.

"Love is a fountain," he whispers.

The floor above and around him has no answer, only the echo of a million footsteps and a thousand squeaking gurneys, the passing of lives in the rhythm of the badly greased wheels and the shuffling attendants with their cigarette breath and sad assignations in the staff locker room after hours.

"Love is a fountain."

Even the air ducts are silent for once.

"What became of her?"

In the endless noise of his dissolution he remembers there is something he cannot face, some face he cannot look at, some look his eyes will not meet. Remembering, he forgets, his scream quiet as ever his passion had been.

"It was a mistake," echoes a voice he might once have recognized, but he is spread too thin to understand what it is he might be hearing.

ii: Love in the Time of Flesh

Pleasantly stoned, Markus followed Danni down the cracked sidewalk. The warehouses seemed larger than they had before, older, more ragged. The walls might have been breathing, he wasn't sure.

She walked close in front of him, her hips swaying in the tight leather pants she favored. Danni was a little woman, lithe, he thought—that was her word, "lithe."

The hippie truck growled to life with a sudden kicking of the starter that startled him. Markus flattened back against the wall, even as Danni laughed without turning around.

It wasn't the noise. No one had climbed into the cab, come or gone from the vehicle.

The truck ground its way into gear with a racket that put Danni's abuse of her Civic to shame, them rumbled away, dragging the concealing tarp the better part of a block before it dropped off. The rear door of the trailer was spray-painted with a slogan in some Cyrillic language—Russian, probably, in San Francisco; like KGB gang tagging.

Then she pulled him into a narrow walkway between two warehouses, along a path through shattered glass, cigarette butts and the corpses of ancient bicycles.

"Visitors' entrance," Danni said. Her voice was almost normal.

"Yeah." Markus wasn't afraid, not exactly, but there was something wrong here. She was daring him to ask, *entrance to what*, but he knew better.

Then they were at a door, plywood boarding up what had once been glass or mesh, painted over in a dozen layers of old color now flecked like a shattered, drab rainbow. Danni shoved her shoulder against the door, bouncing her weight twice, before it sprang open with a screech of strained plywood and protesting nails.

Markus followed her through, his leather jacket snagging on something.

Inside reeked of rot and bandages and things left wet in the shadows far too long. They were in a little office, old furniture crusted with rat droppings and the fluff of asbestos insulation pulled down for nests. The path from outside led into the jumbled sea of water-logged cardboard on the floor and out through a gaping door into the wider warehouse.

As they walked in the mucky shadows, Markus heard a cow lowing.

"What?" he blurted, before stopping himself.

"Daddy Nekko knows what every good boy wants," Danni said.

He could hear her grinning, even in the dark.

They followed the reek of blood and the echo of meaty thumps through the shadowed gloom of the warehouse.

There were low, heavy noises ahead, and a whuffling like the breath of dozens of bodies. Danni pulled aside a curtain of heavy-gauge plastic and they stepped into light.

Cattle stood, roped together with Kryptonite bicycle cables, their mad eyes rolling back in their heads as they wept blood, quivering in the hold of some drug or bovine dream. The cattle were of that breed Markus always thought of as "Oreo cows," with black forequarters, black haunches, and a pale midsection. Three massive men stood around a metal table, a slab really, working with knives and a chainsaw, dismembering one of the cattle. They were naked save for leather thongs, and knee-high fisherman's boots, their skin oiled with the lifeblood of the animal.

One glanced up at Danni and Markus, nodded. His face was covered with a smooth leather mask, only eye slits and little mesh over his mouth granting him human features at all. His head was shaven, with a tattooed map on the scalp. It appeared to be the San Francisco transit system, with its multicolored web of streetcars, buses and rail lines all somewhat at odds with one another.

The other two men had mapped heads as well. He recognized them, one with the London Underground and the other with the Manhattan subway system. All three bent back to their work, sawing and hacking with a sound that stirred Markus' guts.

It was a slaughterhouse. One he was fairly certain had no standing with the city or state authorities.

"Daddy Nekko says you can cut if you want," Danni whispered, running her tongue across his ear. "You can even kill if you want." She reached down, grabbed up a sledgehammer, and pressed it into his sweating hand.

Balancing the handle on his shoulder, Markus stepped forward to watch the cutting. His groin pulsed, penis as hard as it had ever been, as Danni followed behind, slipping her hand down his pants to stroke his butt.

Ego: Questioning

I have to get out of here. I have to make this stop. I have to find Danni . . . no, refind her. Where the hell is she? What the hell happened? I can't feel my hands. I can't feel my feet. I can't see.

I am blind, eye-blind, skin-blind.

I try to scream, but I am mouth-blind as well.

I am not ear-blind, yet.

And slowly I realize that I shall never have the mercy of becoming memory-blind, as much as I might pray for that end.

What have I done? Where's Danni?

I move to explore the extents of my blindnesses. I realize that eye-blindness is not quite right. Bright streaks and specks and silver speckles punctuate my darkness.

Night?

In a ward?

If I could move my head, I could look to see if red and green lights flicker in time to the machine-beeps that surround me. I could interrogate my world. If I could move my head.

But I feel nothing on my body. No cool sheets, no leather straps, no serrated bone knives cutting deep into my receiving flesh. Only my thoughts, only my ears, only my not-quite-seeing eyes.

Where is Danni?

Where am I?

What has become of what I meant to do?

I can remember the second cut, the bigger one, digging a strip from my thigh, working with scalpel and surgical scissors, laying it open so that it would heal in a trough, a divot of the flesh where a lover's fingers might rest, reaching within me, shielded only by scar tissue and old pain from what pulses at my core.

I did that one in the basement, in a galvanized tub filled with water and whiskey, almost four hundred dollars' worth of Very Old Barton pickling me like a well drink in a shitty bar, instant antiseptic, blood staining the water even as I sipped from a little bucket, digging out my flesh the way a child digs sand at the beach, wrapping the strangled strips around my fingers, burning the wound shut with an old blowtorch, and smiling into the bright pain until I knew she would come and finally, finally, finally love me for the sacrifices I have made for her.

Balls to the Wall

The blood flows differently further down the trunk. It spreads, slows, finds its way into crannies of the body, carrying oxygen to places where the Divine Engineer did not think quite so far ahead.

Blood-flow is familiar territory now, and Markus follows the pattern, letting the veins carry him where they will. He knows he is southbound, so to speak, and has his suspicions. Soon enough the red tide carries him into a spinning, curling region where the flow goes round and round and a massive orb rises like a globe of ferrous mercury emerging from an ocean of gelid fat.

"Welcome," says a voice. Where the liver was angry, frustrated, there is an almost divine detachment to this great thing. He realizes that is one of his testes.

He might as well be speaking to the moon.

"Hello," Markus says quietly. He can find suddenly none of his anger or desperation. He only has resignation now.

The moon-voice booms. "We are the seat of love."

"I know," he says. "You are the fountain."

There is a long, slow silence, the noise of something

great passing overhead. "We are not the fountain. That lies elsewhere."

"But love is a fountain."

"Love is everything."

Rote philosophy. He realizes that his testes are not very bright. "What happened to me?" he asks anyway, thinking they might know more than he does somehow. They *are* the seat of love.

"Everything."

Love. The great slow voice means love.

"But what happened to *her*?"

"Who?"

And now, Markus is so far from memory, that he cannot remember. Who was she? Where did she go? How far away did she go?

She led him, he understands suddenly, led him to a place where she left him, abandoned by his guide, deserted by his love, stranded in the blood-red precincts of his worshipping soul.

"Damn," he says.

"Love is not a sin," the moon-voice intones. "There is nothing to damn here."

"Only me," he says, his voice descending into a whimper.

A great tube comes for Markus, elephant's trunk the size of the world-snake, whuffling and snorting, and he is pulled up, transported by the miracles of peristalsis and hydraulics, moving ever faster toward an inevitable end that would have him crying out were he able to cry any more in this life or the next.

He misses what he has lost, he realizes, if only he understood what that would be.

The name comes to him then, a parting gift from the moon-voice echoing up the long, accelerating tube.

"Danni."

Danni.

Danni?

But that's not his name.

Screaming wordless and soundless, he is born once more into the dark light of evening on a fountain of love.

γ: Love in the Time of Metal

The machines have him now. Silicon circuits, copper jumpers, small blocks of bright plastic connected with goo and solder. He chases electrons, tinier than he has ever been, a single-orbited machine reduced to a solitary bit of information about himself, though replicated a thousand million times so that he actually can remember who he is in moments when enough of him cross himself over.

This machine here monitors his heart. He stares out of the winking red eyes at the body on the bed, then flinches without registering what is missing and what is there.

That machine there monitors his electroencephalograms.

Little waves dance, flat then high, swelling across one another in a march of thought and feeling. He would climb and surf, if he could, but metal gleams in the green glow outside his fascia, metal and different colors of flesh, a person underneath a sheet wrapped in bandages that protect those around him.

The *other* machine monitors blood chemistry, a realtime assay of those things which might kill him in a moment. He avoids that as well, avoids the messy truths about blood volumes and types and contaminants, preferring instead to feed into the wiring harnesses and oxygen lines that permeate the hospital walls, chasing data ghosts and old echoes of himself and those around him.

"What became of her?" he queries the circuit breakers, the junction boxes, the security eyes that watch the orderlies steal drugs and feel up the unconscious women.

"What became of her?" he asks the computers, bitter and silent workstations pounded by nurses and pharmacy techs.

Finally he leaves the hospital to ask the world, but the grid is too large for him and slowly, surely, with the inevitability of a landslide in winter, he is drawn back to the chilled muck and metal-laced hell he has made of his body.

She had made.

His guide.

Leading him to the blood springs, then abandoning him there gutted like a fish, though the feel of her fingers in the wound of his thigh is as fresh as some touch which might have passed between them earlier that same night.

"What have I done?" he asks the hospital systems and the patient floor buffers and the stolid morgue refrigerators.

But here are no answers, only a sixty-cycle hum and the long, slow thoughts of silicon and copper, ageing on a different timescale than their human masters or his dying body.

The truth is there, if only he can lift enough of his eye-blindness to see it.

He will find that truth, in memory if not in the world around him.

Somewhere a nurse squeaks across a threshold, coughs her revulsion, and touches his forehead.

Touch.

He has felt touch.

If his eyes worked, he would weep.

History 101

When Markus was seven, his mother moved the family into the house on County Road 61. Markus couldn't quite remember what had happened to his dad, even then, had not even the memory of knowing, but the scent of aftershave and the sandpaper stubble of a hollowed cheek stayed with him as the sole and primary awareness of fatherdom.

Mother, whom everyone including Markus called Sail

after some long-ago childhood episode, had taken her three kids, Markus and his two sisters, and gone into the sticks of Caldwell County, Texas, in the wake of his father's departure. No one cared much but her and her former in-laws, but that was enough for Sail.

The house he remembered vividly. It was a small frame structure, in the time-honored tradition of backwater Texas counties, the wood silvered to the sheen of a book-eating insect, every beam and joist and window just far enough out of true that the eye ached for something logical and simple, sweeping to the post oak trees or the red-clay horizon of the next rise, rather than dwell on the improbable place.

There had been electricity, and running water, though an outhouse was a necessity. Sail arrived with her three children and such worldly goods as could be stuffed into an electric blue 1969 Mercury Marauder with a rusted-out floor pan covered over in bright orange Homasote. Markus' first real memory in life was unpacking that car, toting huge canvas mail sacks of clothing and dishes that all reeked of smoke.

He never did remember a fire.

So they settled into life, five plates and three spoons between the four of them—Sail, Markus, Anna, and Tildy.

Markus first realized something was wrong, in a different way, when the fall came around and Sail wouldn't let him go to school.

"You're not leaving the house," she told him. "Ain't safe

out there." Then she gathered him close to her chest—which was like being hugged by an ironing board—and whispered in his ear, her breath hot with chilis and beer. "Ain't losing my other man to nobody."

Markus wiggled away, slipping out of her scabbed arms to run outside where the bullfrogs peeped and the coyotes yipped. He lay on his back amid misting cow pies and counted stars until his eyes watered from the scent and the evening chill.

When he went back to the house, both of his sisters were sleeping on the porch couch. It had arrived lashed to the roof of the Mercury, and though there was no inside couch, it was still the porch couch. Anna and Tildy were curled up among a pile of feed sacks, rolled together like a pair of puppies.

That likely meant Sail had been smoking, Markus knew. She usually sent the kids outside before she got her pipes out.

He went in anyway, cold and looking for something to drink.

The house was dark, no lights at all, so the sheets over the windows glowed a pale, shiny blue from the moonlight outside. Sail wasn't on the blankets in the front room, so Markus slipped into the kitchen. He very carefully opened the water tap, trying not to set the pipes to banging, and filled a chip-lipped jelly jar. After drinking the water down, Markus stepped quietly back into the front room, only to run into Sail, literally smacking his face into his mother's bare belly.

She was nude except for a blanket over her shoulders like a cape. Markus looked down, away from the dark tips of her breasts, only to find himself staring at the fur between her legs. Sail wrapped her arms around him, pulling Markus close so his face was pressed into her belly again, her breasts nudging the top of his head.

"Oh, my boy, my baby, my baby-man," she whispered. Her arms wrapped tight around him, and she began to move her hips as if she itched.

"Mom," Markus complained, but she drew him down onto the blankets, and curled him so close he could barely breathe, kissing the top of his head over and over and over and calling him by some man's name.

Despite himself, he grew warm and hazy, snuggling in closer to her chalky, sour-milk skin until his mouth found her breast and they both suckled to sleep.

He woke to pain. His mother stood over him, her face red, spitting, still naked, beating at him with a pair of black-handled kitchen scissors. Anna and Tildy were shrieking nearby, but Sail kept slapping him with the flat of the blades, some of the blows cutting him anyway, shrieking

"Pervert! Pervert!" until he rolled away and hid beneath the blankets crying, rubbing the blood of his wounds free with his fingers and suckling the fluid down in the warm salty memory of the night before.

Id: Causative Agent

I will ever be machine. They have wired me tight, filled me with batteries and probes and psychotronic receptors. They have braided my nerves with superconducting filaments wired into the mind of God. They have inserted drills and chisels and silver-belled hammers into my head, making room among the valleys of my cerebellum for their ideas, for their world, for their small minds and smaller needs.

To be machine is to be reduced. To be reduced is to become something both less and more, focused and refined, lost in the spinning axles that bind the axes of the universe together, an agent of change and visualization and ideation loose within the weeping walls of the world.

My machine-self is oiled with blood, a fluid ever more viscous and meaningful than the common run of heartsalt which flows from most wounds. Even an amateur can mainline sewing machine oil, but only the evolved, those in touch with their inner steel and brass, those for whom the concept of valvehood has gone from engineering abstraction to personal integument, can truly understand the reach and breadth of the mechanical man.

Metal does not weep. Iron does not know pain. Brass does not understand fear. Cold electrons carry no unpleasant memories. Hydraulic lines bring no traitor joy, to tempt a man into lying down on another bed of pain.

Machine ever I will be, lost in the twisting coiling guts of flensing knives and rendering fats and great metal forks which twist muscle fibers like yesterday's spaghetti and tomorrow's surplus data cabling mixed together, until all the flesh and pain is drawn forth from me and I have been distilled of purpose, distilled of feeling, distilled of the deep wells which make me human.

Distilled of love.

δ: *Love in the Time of Metal*

He is become a laser. The modern surgeon's blowtorch and machete in one sleek package, cutting and cauterizing and making small and making whole in one ruby beam. He has lost himself in the intricacies of crystal, light, timing, and phase. He knows that if God had a finger on the world, it would be a laser too, a giant beam of ruby death stalking the landscape as dread as any whirlwind. Just as his laser-self stalks the flesh, pushing dread and fear of change before *his* bright finger.

There is an exploration now, a mapping of flesh and outreach toward bone, his bright blade of light slicing someone toward blessèd oblivion. The skin seems familiar, mottled tones and metal interruptions looming before him in a landscape as intimate as any mission-profiled terrain begging for the arrival of daisy cutter munitions and fuel-air explosives.

His laser self traces the scars of old sutures, stumps and pits where such things as a body might need to prosper seem to have vanished from the flesh, traveling on over that tight terrain as intrepid as any explorer of ancient days. He is pleased to note that some of the work is very well done indeed, as if shaking hands had improved skills over time.

Or slim hands had rendered aid, when the shaking hands and missing fingers became too intrusive.

He inquires of a scar: "What became of her?"

The light hisses, photons making impossible noises, as the gears and screws within his lungs begin to jangle together.

"What became of her? Why did she leave me behind?" A pitted scar amid mesh plates on the abdomen has no answer.

Something spasms, big and glittering, looming in the darkness as a doctor curses and the laser that is him stutters. A blade is loose, free, unable to be separated from the flailing arm as the jangling within his lungs fights to become a scream, a sob, a shout of terror.

"Where is she?"

The name comes back again, a gift from some part of his body or another.

"Danni!" he shouts.

There is almost a noise. The laser flickers and dies, the doctor curses again, the landscape of flesh and metal and suture scars writhes more wild while the blade flies free with a spray of someone else's blood and his quiet scream turns to aching laughter.

His voice is back, and he can see.

Colon and Semicolon

This migration is lower and slower, a ponderous movement through great channels of peristalsis and annular musculature. The churn is vasty and deliberate, a different push of fluids than he has felt before. Markus is in a great hall, a sort of cloacal cathedral of the body.

He is suddenly glad to be nose-blind.

This is the final river, the great fall which evacuates the body and cleanses what was before. He has arrived at the colon in his pursuit of love.

"Hello!?" Markus shouts, his voice echoing off the soft walls and the cavern roof. This is a subway tunnel for dank brown cars that might slide southward and outward.

"Can you hear me?"

After the peevish liver and the emotionally detached

testicle, he is not sure what to expect. There is nothing but a deep pipe-gurgle, the world moving around him.

"I'm looking for Danni."

Danni. Who *is* Danni? Not himself.

"Danni," groans a voice, long and slow and low like a pipe organ gone feral. "Danni is here."

For one moment he thinks the colon means that Danni is here inside him. The medical image, the black machine scan of his head in Dr. Thompson's hand, shudders in his vision—a thing to be avoided, a thing to be feared, a thing to possess the mind and worry the body. Like the idea of Danni inside of him.

Has he eaten her?

Who was she?

"Danni," says the voice again. It echoes off the vault of the colon, whispers down the twisted corridors amid the sloshing waste. "Markus. You cut her to the quick, Markus. You wasted her love, Markus. You drove her away trying to pull her too close, Markus."

"No." He argues, knee-deep in unquiet filth. "I did not."

"Love cuts both ways."

Memory: a flash of knives, an arc of blood, laughter on the tight, screeching edge of fearsome madness and maddening fear. Orgasms can erupt from any slit in the body, not just the tips and gashes nature intended.

"We always sewed ourselves shut again," Markus says.

"Seamster. Tailor man." The colon seems distantly amused, almost scornful. "What would you make? You wasted her love. You wasted her."

"I just wanted her close!" he shouts, heart pounding, mind spinning out of control.

"Close." The colon gurgles loud, then settles down. "What is close?"

"Close is love."

"Close is pathology. Stand alone, man, stand alone."

He realizes he is literally arguing with a shithole. "No. I don't want . . . this."

The colon does not seem to resent his opinion. "It is too late to decide what you want."

"It's never too late," Markus grumbles.

Then the wave washes higher and higher, he tumbles downward, outward, southward, flying at speed into the wasteland of futures past.

"You know where she is," the colon echoes after him in a foetid blast.

History 102

The first time Sail sewed Markus with a needle was the night of his tenth birthday.

Most Saturdays she set the girls to sleep on the porch or in the car, if it was cold enough. She kept Markus in the house those nights for their quiet evenings together. That his tenth birthday fell on a Saturday was something Sail saw as a cause for extra celebration.

"I'm sorry you don't have a party, my little man," his mother told him that afternoon. Anna and Tildy sat at the card table with Markus and Sail, the four of them sharing a cake made from oatmeal and molasses, with Crisco and brown sugar frosting.

"I'm sorry, too, Momma," he said, hands folded on the table. A year behind in school, Markus was always too tall, too gawky, too old, too slow, too big.

Too. His entire life was toos.

At least she'd let Anna and Tildy go to school on time. There the three of them were, first, second and third grade, though he should have been in fourth, or maybe even fifth, by his age and size.

The house had changed over the years, too. Sail had taken up painting, mostly on pieces of silk from the Goodwills in Lockhart and Austin, which she sold for enough money for dope and beer and food, in roughly that order.

Saturday nights, if he was good, and good to *her*, Markus got to share the dope and beer.

When she didn't have silk, she painted the walls. Eventually, she stapled bedsheets over the paintings and painted more, but the staples tended to work loose, so that the walls became a billowing, sagging blouse of color and pattern, great abstracted sunflowers and little VW microbuses with almost-Deadhead bears dancing behind them like a Jerry Garcia ulcer dream, crossed with purple-eyed unicorns and louche Aztec maidens with brown-tipped breasts that were all too familiar to Markus, and a dozen other fevered visions beside.

It was like living inside the shipwreck of someone else's imagination.

"Happy birthday to you . . . " the girls sang, as far from key as two little kids ever got. The family mashed their way through the tune, celebrating another year in a life that Markus already saw little point in happiness for.

Later, the girls were outside giggling over dirty magazines in the back of the Mercury. Markus wished he was with them under the blankets, rubbing shoulders and hips and sipping from a wine bottle.

Here inside, Sail leaned over him, her breath smoky with dope.

"I got a present for my little man," she whispered. "His own little works. But you're too young for cousin white, my little man." She showed him a curved needle, almost a half-circle, thick and stout. It was threaded with something that glinted pale in the moonlight. "Hold very still for Momma."

She took his right hand in her left, grip trembling as she shoved the needle into the ball of his thumb. "Let it hurt, little man," his mother whispered, her tongue flickering across his cheek.

He watched unicorns dance in the moonlight and listened to his pain, while his mother's hips twitched as she settled her weight onto him. Somewhere in the middle of it, he heard his sisters laughing outside so loud their voices carried through the windows of car and house alike.

The laughter carried him forward past the peeling rainbows until it was time for dope and beer and slow kisses beneath cool sheets.

iii: Love in the Time of Flesh

Later, bloody, they fucked atop the squelching, rotten boxes in the office. As Markus thrust into Danni's ass, hands gripping her shoulder and hip, another cow died in the slaughterhouse with a bovine scream. He pulled her close, her sphincter dry of anything but his spit and a quick swipe of her cunt, moving slowly so the friction wouldn't tear or hurt. The animal blood on his chest, still warm, smeared on her back. She moaned with the sensation.

"I . . . love . . . you . . . " he muttered with the thrusts. The ends of the bars in her inner thighs met his skin with every push as she wriggled backward into him.

"Fuck . . . off . . . " she gasped back, shivering her orgasm.

So he grabbed her orange hair and pulled hard until she squealed and bucked, pinching his dick tight as she did.

Somehow their screwing dissolved into a fight then, punching and slapping and pinching, until she landed a solid clip across his chin that rolled him back against one of the desks in a shower of asbestos fibers and rat shit.

He lay there, cum oozing from his bloody, shriveled dick. "God, this place stinks."

"Daddy Nekko thought you'd like it," she crooned, tracing her hand across the blood on his chest.

"Fuck Daddy Nekko."

"Daddy Nekko doesn't fuck," she said in a prim voice. "He's gone beyond that."

In the distance the chainsaw stuttered to life, then immediately yowled as it met resistance.

"Who the hell goes beyond fucking?"

"Oh, there are much greater refinements," she said. Her voice was taut, reedy, and thin, as if she were ready to cum again right then. Her hands strayed to the bars in her legs, as if she were going to masturbate just from touching the metal. "You're a cutter, Markus. You know the rush."

"Yeah." Needles and thread, kitchen scissors, a hot glue gun—his whole young life had been filled with the rush, the gift of pain. It was perhaps the greatest thing his mother had done for him—showing him that path through her own guilt and fear.

"Listen . . . " Danni crawled close, her tongue in his ear, her fingernails pinching the same lobe. "You've been wanting to cut for a long time. *Really* cut. What did you learn here, today?"

What had he learned? That flesh parted tough but smooth under the right knife. That joints pulverized beneath a sledge. How to take apart a hip with a chainsaw.

And on the second cow, he'd learned he could cut while the blood was still hot. Learned he could dig, and draw—not just pig skins from the bodega, but on living canvas. Living art. Make it his.

Maybe . . . maybe . . . make it of himself.

The cow's bloody eye had rolled, it had drooled spit and cud and bile, it had whuffled out its pain despite the drugs, while he'd worked, while London and San Francisco had laughed and New York had smoked a PCP-laced joint, until they'd made him crack the head with a sledge so he didn't ruin the meat with stress hormones.

"I learned I can cut," Markus said slowly, and he was hard again. "Cut anything."

Danni grabbed his balls, pinching so hard his vision spotted up and his gut went deep-sick. "Cut you. Show me you can cut you. And I'll show you what I'll do for you."

"What?" he breathed, balanced on a knife-edge between passion and eye-rolling pain.

"Anything at all," she said. "Anything at all."

Later at his place, showered and somewhat clean, they made love in a fashion which was almost distressingly ordinary. Sometimes that felt good, too. Two adults, nude, rolling on a mattress, kissing, fucking, touching, pinching, and slapping a little—no cutting, no pain that meant anything.

Like someone's parents might have fucked.

He wondered what it would be like to have parents who were normal. Went to church on Sunday, went out for drinks on Friday, sent the kids to the Saturday matinee so they could stay home together.

"Hey, Danni," he whispered, lying across her body, both of them spent again.

"Hmm . . . ?"

"Tell me about your family. You know, when you were a kid."

She went stiff, scared or angry. "Get off me, Markus."

"What?"

Danni pushed at him. Small as she was, she pushed hard, then punched his ribs. He rolled away, freeing her.

"I'm going," she told him. "Don't ever ask me any questions again."

"But . . . " He was sorry, very sorry, he'd said anything. "Listen, I didn't mean it."

"I don't ask you *shit*!" she screamed, pulling herself into her leather jeans. Her tiny breasts bobbed as she hopped on one leg then the other. "I never ask you *fuck* about where you came from or who the *fuck* Sail is or why you cum in your sleep while you're crying for some girls I never *fucking* heard of in the back seat of a car somewhere. So how fucking *dare* you ask me *shit* about *shit*, you stupid fucking shit!"

"Danni!"

She pulled her jacket on, not even bothering with her shirt. "I'm outta here, dickbreath. You ever get right with me, you ever get serious, you'll know where to find me. But I'm not holding my breath."

She slammed the door so hard three glasses fell off the counter in the kitchen.

Markus lay there a while, wondering what had possessed him to open his mouth. He didn't want normal. Whatever the hell that meant. People who'd never stepped beyond themselves.

After sitting and thinking for a long time, Markus decided it was time to stop just planning his first serious cut. He went and ran the shower, hot and hard, and found the bull dykes in his tool drawer, with the blue electrical tape on the handle. And some duct tape to bind his foot, along with a big swig of Jägermeister to get him going.

He would mail Danni something she wouldn't forget. Something that would bring her back to him. And fuck Daddy Nekko.

Just fuck him, Markus thought, as he made his way to the steaming edge of the tub, tools in hand.

The Sins of Markus Selvage

Pride

Envy

Gluttony

Lust

Wrath

Greed

Sloth

Fornication

Incest

Mutilation

Masturbation

Self-Creation

Dishonoring the Sabbath

Animal Cruelty

Suicide

Or was it murder?

Superego: Desire

I meant to do it. I wanted to do it. I needed to do it. It became me. It became here.

Consider pruning shears. Nineteen dollars and change down at the hardware store, plus a pair of spiffy rubber gloves with that powdery texture and new-latex smell. Yet they can bring so much pleasure.

After the toe, after the trough in my thigh, Danni

believed. She came back. But she wanted a bigger cut. A real cut. Something she could believe in. Something she could take part in.

We put down forty mil vinyl sheeting, duct taping over my entire living room to seal the floors and baseboards. I brought the blowtorch up from the basement. I bought the pruning shears and gloves, and a lovely duck at the Wing Fat Oriental Market on Guerrero.

Danni and I would dine well.

Then we did it, by God, naked and breathing hard, touching one another's bodies, masturbating one another, her fucking me with the handle of the shears until my ass bled, then me fucking her until she squealed from the hurt, then we set my left hand on the Formica dining table, duct taping it palm-up to the surface except for pinkie and ring fingers—the cut that would be an undeniable public statement of who and what I would become.

The cut that would make her love me forever.

The cut that would bring us together.

The moments before I took the shears in my right hand and did the deed, the moments before my life truly changed, were the most perfect of my existence. My love for Danni, her love for me, balanced in that instant as nothing ever had before, and I suspected, ever would again.

Then the blades closed down on the pinkie joint between my third knuckle and the palm of my hand. The metal cut in hard, the pain shooting through me like an angel's orgasm, and I screamed as she did, until the finger dropped off and a red fountain of blood flowed from the stump, our love mixed together as she slobbered and cried and kissed and climbed up on the tabletop to shove her quivering vagina onto my bleeding hand while I cursed and reached for the blowtorch before I lost too much blood and pain to do the other finger and consummate our love, our pact, who we are and who we might become.

Daddy Nekko: a Transcript

A: "Subject is, uh . . . Daddy Nekko. Is that an alias?"

(crosstalk)

A: "Never mind. Got to be a God-damned alias. Nobody names their kid 'Daddy.' Subject is Daddy Nekko, Asian-American male about fifty years of age, estimate three hundred and fifty pounds . . . can you pull that in for a tight shot? And get someone to look at the weight issue. Jesus, I've seen smaller pianos."

B: (unintelligible) " . . . a shithole, Burris."

A: "Shove it. You want to do this?"

B: "No. I'll go find . . . " (unintelligible)

A: "Offhand, I'd say cause of death is exsanguination due to multiple wounds, but there's also a significant degree of mutilation here. Something like a . . . uh . . . ritual murder, maybe? Most of the parts seem to be present."

C: "I'm not doing the fucking inventory."

A: "I'm working here, you mind?"

C: "Sorry." (cough) "This is creepy shit."

A: "You can always transfer over to fucking parking and traffic."

C: (unintelligible)

A: "You too, pal. Uh . . . Hey, Ransom, do a slow pan of the stiff for me? Good." (long pause) "Setting is a . . . body modification shop. Looks like our boy did a lot of the work. There's a plus-size stool over there next to the tool tray. Maybe he had a customer didn't like the outcome. Need to remember to check the piece count for extras. Our boy was into some . . . weird . . . shit. Ransom, what are those chain things with the razors for?"

C: "I haven't the faintest fucking idea, Burris. Why don't you try them and find out?"

A: "Ass-hat. Take the fucking pictures and shut up."

B: "Hey, there's a wheelchair in here!"

A: "What? Huh. That explains the legs."

B: "Oh, shit. More dead guys, too." (retching) "Oh, Jesus."

C: "My God, look at the size of that thing."

ε: *Love in the Time of Metal*

Knife blade, long gleaming thin horizon of bright pain and beautiful edge, leading him onward into razor edge. Once there was stump, bone-bright beneath the thin-stretched skin, and he knew that if he anchored a titanium bolt just *so* and worked wires in just *there* and used a combat-grade neural interface exactly *here*—black market surplus and wicked costly—he could carry a knife with him everywhere. Anchor cabling and tensioners along the remnants of the radius and ulna, allow the long muscles to bond around the surgical steel tang with the help of a slather of stem-cell prep, and it becomes part of one.

He could love himself, so shiny and sharp and beautiful inside the pain space. He could love himself ever-ready to point the way toward a punctured future at the expense of whoever might move too close, step too tightly inside the circle of his love.

Power is pain, pain is power, and the metal edge is the purest instrument of a mother's love. He becomes the knife, becomes the bolts, becomes the wires, finds his way inward.

(Yet still love is a fountain, not a mass of chilled metal.)

He feels his way toward some other future.

(Danni.)

He knows the pain is not enough, not an end in itself, but merely a means toward something greater. Something higher.

Endorphins.

Adrenaline.

The sorrow and the joy of a deep cut, the washing wall of pleasure, even the simple irritation of healing.

(If God had not meant us to cut, why would He have given us blood that clots and skin that closes over?)

He has lost her, even the knives know that. Dr. Thompson knows where she is, but he does not. The beeping machines know where she is, but he does not. The dank, slow breath of dying around him in the terminal ward carries her name on every rattling exhalation, but he does not know.

Did the knives flash, cutting her up?

(Images of Sail, Momma, crying out her last.)

Did the knives flash, driving her away?

(Images of a small orange-headed woman laughing through fear.)

Did the knives flash, loving her too much?

Did he make too much of himself?

Did he make too much of her?

Deep inside his metal-self, he is not proud of who he is and what he has done. Not the pain—he takes great pride in the arts he has learned—but the use and misuse of love, until she was driven away, taken away, gone away from him, leaving him with nothing more but rattling breath and blindness.

Except his ears have returned, and his eyes.

Maybe his skin-blindness will lift soon, and he will know true pain.

Daddy Nekko died hard. He smiles at that, for what the fat man did to her, to his love.

Everyone who hurt his love, hurt in the way that counts, not the way that pleasures, will die hard.

That is why he is here, in this place, the tiny gears and motors of him grinding to empty dust amid the chaos and pleasure of a hospital ward where the nurses' shoes squeak and the children sob endless agony and the very electricity in the walls knows the names of the dead.

He surrenders, then, to his machine destiny, and loves himself, knives and gears and all, finds what he will in the wires within, leaving behind his fear on the garlic breath of the nurse and in the whimpering fellowship of his ward.

And the machines go beep, beep, beep, beep, counting out the measures and rhythms of his life in slow quatrains.

He wonders what his mother would say of her little man now.

The Lung March

He wafts on a column of air, a fairy feather floating on a spring wind to spin high above a blanket-pink landscape of tiny tendrils and distant forests.

Pink?

There is a shudder, a sort of seizure of the world, and the wind shifts with a suddenness that seems like it should have been expected. The air blowing back toward him is dank, warm, smelling of tight places with organic heat, slightly stale. Markus feels stretched, spare in that new wind, wrapped around himself like old blankets on a vagrant's dog.

Then the wind shifts again, cool, the spring returned, and he knows he is moving inward to the lungs, carrying his question and his quest to the great bellows which drive the air into his blood and breeze into his voice.

This is a dark cathedral, thousands of naves and narthexes branching outward and downward and wide and narrow, as if God had grown a million fingers and wriggled them all inside a meat-sponge at once in the process of crafting His creation.

Alveoli.

The word comes to him, unbidden, from some distant memory.

He has never cut lungs. Like cutting guts, the risks seemed close to suicidal. Muscle tissue is one thing, parting sweet skin like the zipper on a child's jacket, but organs.

"Yes," whispers someone, but the word is lost in the gale of noise which follow almost instantly. "We have been expecting you."

If the north wind had a voice, it would be this, raging and clawing at him with empty fingers that scrub his scalp, echoing in his ears like a woman shouting from the bottom of a well.

"I am here," Markus announces.

"We are the bellows that move the engines of life."

"The fountain of love?"

"No." The lungs seem regretful. As if the fact that even their great, slow powers are not enough should be a subject of mourning.

"Danni is here somewhere. I lost her, lost my love." *Cut her away*, he thinks, but he will not say that here, not say that now.

"Nothing is ever lost forever." A certain air of spongy, pink satisfaction creeps back into the lungs. "The air brings all things back to us in time."

"You live in cycles," Markus protests. "Like the heart. For you the entire world has a rhythm of departure and return. A sameness."

"Of course. How else should it be?"

Sitting now on the rounded edge of a bronchiole, Markus reflects on life's patterns. Love is always easier to lose than to find. Pain for love is pleasure, pain of loss is . . . pain of a different sort. And the loss of love is unbearable.

He remembers his mother, sitting there in the inconstant breeze. She had been warm and pink, too, in her ways, and somehow she had loved him, though Markus is not now sure how that was.

"She will come back to you," the lungs say with a sigh the size of horizons.

"No. I have lost her." Markus knows this now, that Danni is gone, this thing his body is trying to tell him.

"She is not lost to you. She is close, closer than you know."

Even the lungs hear, he realizes, the resonance of the chest granting them powers denied to the fatty organs jostling within his abdomen.

"Your wisdom is not mine," Markus announces, realizing he must seek elsewhere for his lost love.

There is a spasm then, another quake of the world, a cough to expel his foreign self at speed into the wider expanses of squeaking nurses' shoes and pilfering orderlies and the cold echoes of machines that are not pink, that are not soft, that do not round themselves to his contours and blades and the bright spiked corners of his love.

History 103

When Markus was thirteen, he went on his first date.

Momma was so proud. She bathed him herself in a big galvanized tub in the middle of the kitchen, while Anna and Tildy ran in and out of the room with different combinations of clothing and accessories, giggling at his nudity until Sail sent them outside to feed the chickens for a while.

He stood, staring up at the pressed tin ceiling which sagged like one of those square-sectioned chocolate bars left too long in the sun—if chocolate was the color of old cream mixed with rust and, somehow, bird crap. Sail's familiar hands ran up and down his body, brushing over the scars on his chest and back and butt, gently scrubbing his penis with a rough rag that made him stiff in spite of his embarrassment.

"My little man isn't going to do anything to get himself in trouble, is he?" she asked, still touching him.

"No, Momma."

"What do you say if she asks about any of your little *accidents*?"

I say I'm thirteen and I don't have to have accidents *anymore*. But he didn't open his mouth.

And besides, those accidents could feel so nice.

"Exactly," Sail whispered. "You gonna be good, Markus?"

"I'll be good, Momma."

"Then let's make sure you've got the right clothes. Where the hell are them girls?"

Later she dropped him off at the Dairy Queen in Lockhart, then took the girls to a movie. Markus wondered where Sail had gotten enough money to take three people to the movies, but with his mother, anything was possible.

He had twelve dollars and forty-two cents of his own, saved from odd jobs and sheer begging from his grandparents on the rare occasions he saw them.

Enough money to buy him and Suzie Elle Petty burger

baskets, and maybe Dilly® Bars. Markus hadn't had a Dilly® Bar in years, hadn't even had a restaurant meal in months and months. He was really looking forward to it.

The Dairy Queen was all red and white and chrome, like something from when cars had fins and everybody's hair was oiled back. He stood near the jukebox, waiting, watching, not wanting to get in line and order anything by himself. The smell of frying oil and ice cream tugged at his gut, making his mouth water at the same time as his stomach almost turned.

Nerves, Markus told himself.

Suzie Elle would be a normal girl.

That thought made his knees turn to jelly.

Markus' date arrived forty minutes late with two other girls and three boys. They tumbled out of a dualie pickup driven by one of the boys, Billy Hardegree—who'd got a hardship license the day he turned fifteen.

"Oh," Suzie Elle said when she pushed in the door of the Dairy Queen.

"He's still *here*!" giggled one of the other girls. Sandy McMann, eighth grade, Markus noted.

"I was . . . just leaving." He spit the words out like teeth knocked loose in a fight.

"Come on," Suzie Elle said, grabbing his elbow and tugging him outside. There was a breeze carrying the scent of distant cattle and fields of milo. "Look, Billy called . . . you know how it is. And you don't have a phone, *Markie*."

"I'm . . . I'm sorry." He wanted to slide beneath the gravel of the parking lot, scuttle away with the rest of the insects.

"Oh, stop it," she said. "Wait for me, a little while." She glanced around. "Down the street by the library. The porch at the side door. Where they won't see you. I'll be back."

An hour passed. Markus watched his mother drive by looking for him, watched Anna run into the Dairy Queen twice, before they gave up and the rusted old Mercury headed back out into the county. He kept his back against the bricks and his face in shadow.

No one noticed him, not even his family. It was a long walk home, to County Road 61, but he really, really wanted to meet up with Suzie Elle again.

Billy's dualie truck finally roared to life, then departed bearing blonde hair and laughter and tight sweaters. A minute or so later Suzie Elle walked across the gravel, up the library lawn, and joined him in the shadows. She put her arms around his neck.

"Listen," she said. "A kid like you with someone like me. You know how that works. I couldn't show my face at school. Except I heard you got . . . um . . . *experience*?"

Who would know that? he wondered.

His sisters, of course. A grade behind, sixth and fifth to his seventh.

"Uh . . ." Markus couldn't think what to say. "Yeah." Some. His groin was warm, his dick pushing against his pants.

"Billy and me been . . . fooling." She put her head into his neck, her breath hot against him. "He's an idiot. Don't know what he's doing. You show me, I can show him."

Despite himself, Markus' hands strayed to her back, sliding down to her hips.

Just like Momma liked to be touched.

"Where?" he whispered.

"Blankets in the ditch over at that stand of trees behind Main and Bee," she said, slipping her fingers into the front of his pants.

A bit later, when he pressed her hard, she just whimpered. When he hit her, she moaned. He wished he had scissors, or needles, but her teeth were enough.

A deputy sheriff drove up to their house a week following. The brown and gold Crown Victoria idled in the driveway behind Sail's old Mercury as a very fat man in a tan uniform got out. He carried a nightstick in one hand.

Markus walked outside, ready to throw up. "Momma's sick." Stoned out of her mind, actually, naked on the living room floor. "Can I help you?"

"Mark Selvage?" the deputy said.

"Yes, sir."

"I need to speak to your mother. And you're going to have to come with me."

"Why?"

The deputy's eyes got narrow, piggy, angry. "You whupped the shit out of that girl when you raped her, son. And now she's pregnant."

The nightstick swung fast and hard, catching Markus on the elbow. He collapsed, sucking in his breath with the pain.

"You resisting arrest, boy?" the deputy asked, leaning close, beer and beef on his breath. "Answer me right now."

Markus tried to find his voice, but the pain had flattened his lungs.

Another blow, to the ribs, so hard something cracked inside.

"Don't try to run away from me, boy. Shouldn't ought to do what you did to that poor girl."

A kick this time, in his hip.

"We'll take *good* care of you down at the lockup. Couple of days to get you to juvenile, I'm sure." He leaned close, jowls flapping. "Next time, don't fuck with the county judge's niece." A tap on the forehead, almost gentle. "So where's that pretty little mother of yours, boy?"

Anna screaming from the porch interrupted them. After that, Markus just stared at the sky for a while, until he was dragged in the back of the Crown Victoria, his head slammed in the door twice, then driven off over bumps larger than he was, the way they made his mind bounce off skin and blood and memory.

iv: Love in the Time of Flesh

"It's time for you to meet Daddy Nekko," Danni said. She was licking the scabbed-over stump of his left pinkie, the two of them spread out on the plastic sheeting he hadn't bothered to pull up in the weeks since taking his finger.

Markus whimpered with the intensity of the feeling. Like rock salt being grated into skin, or vinegar and whiskey on an abrasion. "I don't know," he whispered.

"You owe him." Danni's teeth closed over the corner of his hand, as if she'd swallowed his finger. He almost came with the sensation.

"Yeah." Without Daddy Nekko, he wouldn't have gone to the slaughterhouse. Without the slaughterhouse, he wouldn't have found his way to . . . wherever he was now. With Danni. With the pain.

The bars in her thighs clattered together as she twitched. "You'll love him."

Maybe, Markus thought. Love was an elastic concept.

Then her teeth clamped on the bones inside his hand and new pain blossomed, within the healing wound and inside the flesh of his palm, and he felt closer, tighter, more bound to her.

Another gear-grinding, head-banging ride through San Francisco. This time they were somewhere up near Golden Gate Park, a neighborhood that reeked of mortgage bankers and low-end venture analysts. Old ornamented houses overhung tiny garage doors, and Markus couldn't have parked a Vespa on this street.

Danni simply slid the Civic into a driveway, nudging it sideways up to an overhead door to completely block the sidewalk. "Come on," she said brightly. "He's waiting."

"I was expecting something like the slaughterhouse."

"Daddy Nekko is different."

They hopped out of the car, scuttled across the street and up a stone stair to a front door paneled in beveled, frosted glass, as ornate as anything Markus had ever seen. Danni pushed the door open without knocking. Markus followed her in to a front hall that was classically San Francisco. A Tiffany lamp dangled from a chain, patterned silk lined the walls, and a collection of unusably delicate furniture was scattered around, crystal bowls filled with candy and a tall vase overflowing with rusted razorblades.

"Ah," he said.

"Downstairs."

"Do they know . . . ?"

"Of course."

She led him through a parlor done in the same style

as the entryway, then down a flight of stairs into another world.

The basement was tiled like a morgue out of the 1950s, all linoleum and stainless steel wall panels, with rubber mats underfoot. Massive surgical lamps nodded like hugely distended heads over a pair of slab tables complete with blood gutters. There were instrument trays standing by, covered with shrink-wrap. Stainless shelving on the walls featured an astonishing array of blades, metal objects, prostheses and electrical devices.

No one was in the room.

Danni stopped with a sigh that sounded like the smallest of orgasms. "Isn't it beautiful?"

This antiseptic splendor was almost exactly the opposite of the slaughterhouse, Markus realized, a post-modern empire of blood and pain conquered with surgical precision and obsessive cleanliness.

The bald man with London on his head stepped backward through a swinging door, still naked save his thong. He was pulling the largest wheelchair Markus had ever seen, and swiveled it around without a word or a glance of recognition to reveal the largest man Markus had ever seen. An enormous Asian.

Daddy Nekko. Four hundred pounds if he was an ounce, the pale color of an antacid tab, like a Samoan with jaundice, naked as an Oregon pole dancer, skin blank as any ink virgin. His eyes were tiny in the folds of his face, fleshy and piggy as a deputy sheriff, and his teeth were stained scarlet as he smiled.

"Da'i," he said, with a voice like a mouth full of oatmeal. Even from across the room, Markus could see there was something wrong with Daddy Nekko's tongue. "We'co'."

"Daddy Nekko." Danni bowed her head, twitched as if she wanted to kneel. "Thank you for seeing us."

"Thi' i' Ma'kuth."

It was a statement. Markus was pretty sure Daddy Nekko didn't ask a lot of questions. "Yes, sir," he said. "Thank you for seeing us."

The chair ground across the floor toward them. "Le' me th'ee your 'and."

Markus held out his left hand. The scab where his finger had been glistened, kept loose and damp by Danni's ministrations.

Daddy Nekko took Markus by the wrist, turning the hand over, back and forth. Then he snapped his fingers and held up his own free hand. London handed him a dental pick. Daddy Nekko began probing the skin around the scab as Markus winced, trying not to twitch. Then the fat man stabbed straight into the scab.

Markus couldn't hold his pain behind his teeth. "Ha . . ."

"Goo' nerve denthi'y." Daddy Nekko glanced up, his

tiny eyes catching Markus' gaze in a vise. The fat man's whites were as red as his teeth. "You cu' goo'."

"Thank you, sir."

Nekko glanced at Danni. "I can 'o i'."

"Markus," Danni said slowly. "I want you to trust me now. Really trust me. Daddy Nekko can take you beyond . . . anything. Even what we already share. But you have to follow him. Without questioning. For the love of me, will you let him do what needs to be done next?"

Sail flashed in Markus' head, his week face-down in the Caldwell County jail, those summer nights with his sisters—all the years and blood and pain of his life. Was he waiting for this?

What *was* he waiting for?

Everything with Danni was a plunge, from one unknown to the next, following the pain.

"All right."

London led Markus to one of the tables, pulled out leather straps, and fastened down his entire body. The nodding-head lamp was brought low over him, light at the height for someone in a wheelchair, but blinding to Markus even through closed eyes. Daddy Nekko rolled up beside him.

He heard metal clink, a drill whine twice as it was tested, then soft giggling and sound of kissing.

Danni and London, making out on the other operating table, as probes began to dig into his hand. When Markus began to scream, every pressure he'd ever felt erupted like steam from an overfired boiler, until his voice eventually fell raw.

The Death of Sail Selvage

Lockhart Post-Register, Thursday, December 9th

Page One (above the fold)

HEADLINE: Caldwell County Woman Brutally Murdered

COPY: Sail Selvage, residing on County Road 61 in the Chamberlain Tract, was found dead Monday morning by her grown daughter, Anna Forksmith of Red Rock. Ms. Forksmith called 911 at approximately seven a.m. in a hysterical state, reporting that her mother had been murdered. Caldwell Sheriff's Office spokesman Kathy Clarke says that investigations are still ongoing and they currently have no suspects.

Ms. Selvage's son Markus was in trouble with law repeatedly during his school years here in Caldwell County, but he is believed to now be residing in California. The Sheriff's Office reports that California authorities are cooperating with the investigation.

"Ms. Selvage kept to herself as far as we can tell," Clarke stated, "and didn't have any enemies or grudges. There are some unusual characteristics to this crime that I'm not at liberty to discuss that should aid in identifying the perpetrator."

Persons with information pertaining to Ms. Selvage or her son, especially his whereabouts, are urged to contact the Sheriff's Office as soon as possible.

"Son always was a bad little motherfucker," said Deputy Morrison, remembering a fall day more than ten years earlier when he'd taken the shit-ass punk in. He began laughing at his own joke, in a sort of snickering cough.

"Yeah." Clarke took a deep drag on her Natural American Spirit cigarette. They weren't as good as quitting, but they beat Marlboro.

The two of them sat on a red picnic table outside the old folks' Dairy Queen near the library.

The deputy laughed once more. "Cut her up bad."

Clarke felt queasy. Jesus Christ, was she pregnant again? "Yeah."

"Never seen nothing quite like it."

"No shit, Bert." She blew smoke at him. "Why don't you go whack off over it, then come back and tell me again?" More smoke. "No, wait! You already did!"

Morrison shifted his weight, turning his hips away. "Whole family was bad. Old man Selvage was right to cut them off after what she did to his Freddie."

"Freddie was the worst asshole in town."

"Hey!"

Clarke shrugged. "Don't care if you two ran together

in high school. You never did like it that Freddie banged Sail and you didn't."

"Don't matter now." Morrison exuded a sort of smug, churchy satisfaction. "She's dead and that boy's gonna be."

"Yeah."

Another cigarette drag, then she was down to the butt burning her fingers. "Look, Bert, just fuck off."

Morrison shrugged and went inside for another milkshake. Clark stared at the pale sky and wondered what would draw such a fucked-up kid back after all these years. Considering the stories, if *any* of it was true, and she was Markus Selvage, she'd have stayed as far away from Caldwell County as humanly possible for the rest of her life.

But somebody had done Sail Selvage real bad, both before and after killing her. Knife, chainsaw, the works. And a lot of needlework, before she died. They were keeping that quiet for now. Let the fucking public defender find out on his own when the time came.

Ego: Regret

I am starting to remember Danni now. She is pretty, smiling with a mysterious air—as if she knows secrets the rest of us cannot even guess at. She is petite, with the kind of build that men and women both turn to watch as she walks down the street in tight leather with just a little too much skin showing. She has metal in her thighs, and metal in her labia, and metal in her nasal septum, and a dozen other places.

She is very much about metal, the Danni I remember, though as she says the metal's just a souvenir, the pain's the thing.

She loved me. Once, for a while, maybe longer. I can't remember yet when that ended, but I regret it. I am not proud of what I have done. Whatever I have done. But she loved me, and I loved her.

I wanted to be close. She led me into countries of pain and love which I had never thought existed. I craved the intensity, the wells of experience she drew me so far into.

What did I do? Why did I do it? Where has she gone?

Some of my blindness is gone. I am no longer eye-blind, though shadows dog my vision like hounds on a dying raccoon. My ears never did stop, or the lying, whispering nurses would have vanished. My head twitches now when I wish to turn it. Soon I will see.

But I am still skin-blind. I think I am still heart-blind, though this slow seep of regret like tar in California sands would seem to be the same as dawn creeping through a drawn shade into the last day of a junkie's life.

There is so much I cannot feel now. Danni's presence, like a spark in the corner of my vision, is dark. My own hands and feet. Even the rattling gears and springs in my lungs seem soft, dying, rotting into old cartilage and from there to a sort of nothing-mucus, a phlegm that is the basic block of my being.

I will find it here before I die, before my lungs rot out of my chest, before my eyes collapse into pools of surprised color. I will face whatever it is that scares me in Dr. Thompson's medical scans, whatever it is my own body denies me in my inward voyages.

I will count the love and the blood and the deaths, and the sum of my life shall be greater than zero, greater than the mark of the razor on the eyeball, greater than the regrets for those things which should have been.

"Where is Sail?" I ask, surprised at my voice, and around me, the air stirs, dying oldsters answering in slow breaths.

"Love . . . "

" . . . is a . . . "

" . . . fountain."

Danni. I meant Danni. Where are you, Danni? I remember you, but you are gone from me.

"Love," the ancient lungs creak, until I lose myself in time and the metronome of uncaring machines that watch over whatever is left of me.

I am sorry, I think, *for whatever I have done.*

History 104

When Markus was seventeen, his sisters came to him.

"Look," said Anna, just fifteen and bursting out of her

t-shirt. Tildy would probably be shaped like Sail—thin and leggy—but Anna had somehow gotten the opposite gene.

"Yeah?" Markus had his feet out the passenger side window of the old Mercury. It didn't run any more, they had a pickup now, but the car continued to sit in front of the house on tires mashed flat by summer heat and relentless time. It was spring and the three of them still needed blankets. His head was on Tildy's lap, and Anna leaned over from the front seat.

"Billy Hardegree's been fucking with me." Anna's eyes flickered toward Tildy. "Us, really, but *someone* doesn't want to bitch."

Markus listened to a cowbird squawk outside, watched the ragged top edge of a post oak barely visible from where he was lying, while Tildy smoothed his hair without saying anything.

Anna spoke for both sisters a lot. In his experience, Anna did a lot of things for both sisters.

"And . . . ?" Markus didn't go around Lockhart High. He hadn't been in school, not really, since the whole rape thing. There had been tutoring in juvie, but somehow the idiot defender on his rap had gotten DNA testing on the tissue samples from Suzie Elle's abortion—and of course there had been no match to him at all.

Nobody had bothered to test Billy Hardegree. They'd just let Markus out of juvie with a buttload of threats and his signature extracted on a bunch of disclaimers and quitclaims.

"Everybody over at the school thinks you eat babies for breakfast and kill spics to keep in practice."

"Mexicans," said Markus heavily. "They're fucking *Mexicanos*. Not fucking spics." He drank at a migrant bar out on the county line.

"So . . . if you come round and make nasty to Billy Hardegree, he'll quit fucking with me." She glanced at Tildy again. "*Us*."

"Last time I had anything to do with Billy Hardegree, I got gang-raped by four drunks in a holding cell while the cops went out for coffee. Then I spent a year in juvie. What the fuck makes you think I want to ever see his sorry ass again?"

Anna pulled her shirt up. She wasn't wearing a bra, and her tits rested on the top of the front seat. He could see a big red mark on her right breast—teeth. Someone had bitten her good. "Fucker got me down behind the bleachers and did this through my t-shirt. Promised me more. You going to let him?"

He reached up and touched the red mark. "Tildy?"

"Grabs my ass in the hall," she said shortly, still stroking his hair. "Thinks he owns us."

"Okay. I'll talk to him."

Sail was drunk again, so Markus didn't have any problem taking the truck the next morning to drive the girls to school. His mother wasn't awake enough to remember that the girls took the bus. He'd wrapped an axe handle in duct tape, tucking it behind the seat, and had his jackknife in his pocket. Tildy sat between him and Anna, her hand on his thigh as he drove.

"Listen," Markus said. His hands hurt where he'd spent a lot of the evening passing a straight razor back and forth over them, stressing the skin and veins without ever quite cutting. "When we get there, I'm staying in the truck. You guys stand around in front of the school 'til he turns up. If he don't, well, go to class and I'll think of something else."

Tildy kissed him on the ear.

The gravel roads hissed them toward town until they hit blacktop, then they cruised faster, pushing seventy, Markus topping the hills like he thought the old Chevy would take flight.

The parking lot of Lockhart High was crammed with Austin-bound SUVs, country pickups and the scattered economy cars of students and teachers everywhere. The school itself was a forgettable collection of pebble-finish slab buildings surrounded by tan trailers with window unit air conditioners. Markus drove through the bus loop and stopped right in front of the school, ignoring dirty looks from the drivers. Anna and Tildy got out and made a show of standing by a planter full of dried dirt, chatting.

Like clockwork, Billy showed up. He walked between the girls without ever glancing at Markus in his truck, draped an arm across each shoulder, and began talking.

Markus got out with his axe handle, walked over to Billy. Three paces back he braced the handle low, and stepping into the blow, swung it up hard between Hardegree's legs from behind.

Billy dropped like an ox as other students began to shriek. Markus leaned the handle into the seat of Billy's jeans and pressed, twisting it, threatening to tear the denim and jam it in the other boy's ass.

Then he leaned down low.

"Last time you fucked with me, I took it up the butt from four mean drunks for a whole evening. Fuck with my sisters any more and you're gonna fucking wish it was only four drunks." He tossed the axe handle away, pulled his knife, slit both of Billy's nostrils and notched the ear he could reach, while Hardegree cried and pissed himself.

Tildy leaned over and spit on Hardegree's face, then the girls went to class.

Markus closed his knife, pocketed it, and walked away before anyone could work up the nerve to tackle him. He left his sisters and his momma's truck behind, and eventually, left Texas behind with them.

v: Love in the Time of Flesh

Markus had never quite passed out, but the pain had pounded him like surf against the shore until he had moved into some other state entirely. So when he finally came to himself, sitting in Danni's car, he was surprised.

"How are you?" Her voice was low, silky, smooth—loving.

"Oh, God . . ." All the cutting he'd ever done, on himself or anyone else, was nothing compared to going under Daddy Nekko's scalpels.

"Do you like it?"

It what? He looked at his left hand, where the pain had been. Was.

A stubby hypodermic protruded from the stump of his knuckle. Sutures and clamps bound it to a ring of skin that Daddy Nekko had constructed, to hold it on.

"What?"

"Wiggle that finger," Danni said.

Markus tried to visualize wiggling the missing finger. Something popped, and there was a feeling of pressure. Three drops of blood oozed from the exposed needle tip.

"Neural interface. Now you can stick me, and we can *share*." She grinned like sunrise over the Sierras. "Welcome to the world of metal, Markus. *Real* metal."

Real metal. He couldn't feel it—the syringe wasn't really

a part of him that way, but there was a valve or something inside he could control.

He couldn't feel it, and it couldn't feel for him. Pain for pleasure. And nothing to hurt inside.

"Oh, God," Markus whispered again. He could only begin to visualize what this would mean. "I can be anything."

"*We* can be anything."

Woozy and hurt as he was, he turned to kiss her as she drove, jabbing the needle deep into the flesh above her collar bone, flexing his vanished finger until their blood mingled and they were really, truly, forever united, at least in that moment.

After the first operation, there was time of delightful variation. They experimented with external routing of venous tubing. Danni implanted a neural interface below his right elbow, which they trained to trigger drills, pumps, even a food processor just for the hell of it.

He felt more human than he'd ever been, more in charge of who and what he was and what he might become. Danni was with him on the voyage of discovery, making big plans for his hands, his feet, his face.

Together they would remake Markus Selvage as someone greater than he'd ever been, someone whole and loved and loving, with the aid of metal where the only pain was to the good and the heart never bled.

The fountain of their love, the spray at the heart of their world, was the blood streaming from the tip of the finger-needle Daddy Nekko had given him.

One day Markus turned to Danni over stewed rabbit with Chianti at his stained Formica table. "When do we take from you?"

"Me?"

"You've got metal in you, but . . . this . . . " He waved his finger, the hypodermic under a leather safety glove, sort of like a little red condom. "You were right. You asked me to do this. I'm asking you to join me."

"I . . . " She stared at her bowl of stew for a moment. "I'm happy where I am."

"So you push me, but you won't follow?" He wasn't angry, just feeling a sort of cold confusion in his chest.

"It's not that simple for me." She looked up at him. "You live in this little apartment, you work in a weirdo bookstore with a bunch of Gothy science fiction types. They don't care about your red fingerglove. I live in the world, sometimes. Front for Daddy Nekko. Can't be missing big pieces of me."

"I see." Though he didn't. When had the risks become all his? Where had they parted ways? Had she wanted only to watch him be sliced away?

Just like Momma, he thought. *Just like Momma, push all the pain on someone else.*

"Come close," he whispered, slipping his fingerglove free, "and kiss me tight."

She glanced at the needle. "Later . . . ?"

"Later?"

Later.

Life was full of laters. He wanted now.

Markus pushed himself away from the table. Thinking of his mother, he went to his room, locked the door, and masturbated, letting the needle poke his dick and his groin over and over until he passed out from blood loss without ever cumming, wondering—until his thoughts grew too dim—what had ever happened to Sail Selvage.

ζ: *Love in the Time of Metal*

"Love is a fountain," he says. His voice has returned. "It pumps and pumps and gives and gives, without limit, without end."

The machines do not answer him. A gurney squeals in the hallway, bearings clogged with pubic hair shavings or the threads from old bandages. The others on his ward breathe their ragged chorus.

"Love is not a mistake," he tells his fellow breathers. They are still human, he presumes, sole and solitary within their flesh, excepted from his heart-armor of invulnerability.

He is more.

The blade that is his left hand moves, twitching with a

life seemingly of its own. A column of flesh and bone is bound to it like the wrapping on a hilt, ending in a syringe, his first and somehow best change into what he has become.

The window frames rattle, air pressure moving outside, the breath of the world matching his breath. He sees the acoustic tile in the ceiling, wiring conduit stapled back and forth like the tubing which might carry blood from one body to another. He sees the flickering of overhead lights, turned down for the night, just bright enough to keep the nurses from tripping as they pass the bulking machines which envelop the dying. He sees the pale glow of the machines around him, green and red constellations, traffic lights for the departing souls.

Markus has watched enough souls depart, though not yet his own. Now, filled with gears and circuits and comforting shafts of cold, hard metal, surgical bolts in his joints and wires in his musculature, he has armored his soul against damage, against injury, against departure.

He is ready to face what has become of Danni's soul.

At that thought, at that moment, he begins to retch, coughing and choking until vomit comes forth, tiny fragments of metal rattling to the floor with his bile and his mucus, the coils in his head unwinding until the nurses come running, followed by orderlies and technicians and eventually a doctor, the mass of white-coated wisdom picking through the pan and marveling at the bright sharpnesses he seems to be producing endlessly from within until he threatens to flood the room and drown them all in razor cuts and slowly, slowly, with each cough and muscle tearing, he remembers what he has done.

What has become of Danni.

"Love is a fountain," he tries to tell them, but his mouth is filled with metal shavings and servomotors. "Love is not a mistake."

"Mistake," whisper the pale-eyed nurses. "Mistake," shout the greedy-mouthed orderlies. "Mistake," intones the sepulchral doctor. "Human," shout the machines in their shrieking, beeping voices as he retches forth yards and yards of cabling.

Markus Selvage: An Inventory
   Syringe, left pinkie
   Cabling, embedded in right forearm musculature
   Cabling, embedded in left upper arm musculature
   Kevlar mesh, rib cage
   Knife, eight inches, mated to stump of left wrist parallel
to remnants of hand, with Kevlar sheath
   Titanium plates, cheekbones, ribs, miscellaneous
   Steel spurs, elbows
   Piercings, various and substantial
   Internal/soft tissue implants, unknown
   Biologica, various and substantial

⇥

Softly Into the Cerebellum

Markus knows this journey by now. He is passing through a swift, rich flow of blood, frothy oxygen being transported toward some higher place, under pressure against gravity, time and entropy. The cycle of the flow tells him he is heading northward, toward his body's hyperborean regions, things coming to a head.

There is a barrier ahead, a stretchy curtain sealing the increasingly tiny channels through which he travels from his road of red. He reaches out, snagging that curtain, leaving the flow to wrap himself in soft gray, fog spun to textile, the death of hope distilled to a caul that could drape across the weeping face of a wretched man.

It is but a step and a twist to pass through the barrier into the complicate, tessellated, tesseracted hallways of the brain.

Biology by Escher. Quantum spaces and open connections, potential drawn forth from the dance of dendrites and the nattering neurons. The stairway which loops back on itself, climbing forever, uphill in every direction, the human mind an island of negative entropy—and here he is within the seat of his own thoughts and feelings like Arthur on his marble hilltop throne in Avalon.

"Where is the fountain?" Markus asks himself.

There is no answer, only the echoing of his whisper within the great halls of mind.

She is here. She is close. Either Danni herself or the memory of her. He is not certain which, nor even certain if there is a difference between her presence and her memory. Is the idea of her the same as her? Is the image of his love for her the reality?

He tries again. "Where is she?" It is like speaking to a well. There are no answers save the quiet whisper of distant, damp echoes.

"What have I done with her?"

The image of Dr. Thompson's scan comes to him unbidden, a memory of that dark, negative image with its curiously squared cheeks.

The plates he sewed into place, pushing them through slits while leaning in front of the bathroom mirror.

But there was something else, something cold and wrong with that scan. Something he could not face. Something fearful.

Something he had done.

"I killed her," he tells his brain.

"I loved her," his brain replies in the voice of a thousand books burning, a crackling, hot narrative that reduces words to ash and scorches his sense of himself.

"She is dead."

"No."

"No?"

"Yes," his brain says.

Many people are dead now. Sail. Daddy Nekko. Two of the map boys. Soon, all too soon, Markus himself most likely, due to complications of tissue rejection.

Tissue rejection?

But he was about pain, and metal.

"Skin so close, skin so fine," his brain tells him, again in that book-voice, the words screaming agony.

"Did I kill Momma?" he asks.

"That's where it began," his brain tells him.

"Where does it end?"

"Here. Soon. Go find the fountain of love."

"Where?"

"Within you. Without you. Wherever you have placed it."

He is sick then, sick of riddles and dreams and half-answers from inside himself. All he wants is Danni, his love back, his truth back.

Somewhere outside him people clothed in white are shouting, bringing great, enormous needles from shrink-wrapped trays, muttering obscenities to the blinking green lights that monitor the passing of his life.

What is it that he cannot face? Inside his head. Inside his body. Inside his brain.

He is cast out in that moment, cast forward, 'til he opens his eyes, opens his mouth, sees the needle buried in his chest and shouts in a voice the size of mountains, "I did not kill her!"

Superego: Resignation

I am finished. I know that now. My attempts to build myself to strength, to a mighty fortress of love, have come to nothing. I have brought too many with me to this final place, a trail of souls behind me.

I will not shrink, nor shirk from these things my hands have done, but neither will I suffer for the sins of others. Sail is at peace, though she did not die peacefully. I did not send her on that final journey, though in another time and place I might have. Daddy Nekko I did send, along with two of his map boys, for what he did to Danni, and through Danni, to me.

Danni . . .

I am sorry for Danni.

The machines have me now. Not my machines, not my beloved metal and electronica, blade edge and blood plasma, but the machines of allopathic medicine, cutting the body without regard to the soul, operations of the flesh that take no account of the wounds of the heart.

Here, now, I am done. My breath rattles. I am not sorry for who I am. I have found love, if only for a while. I am only sorry for her, for all the hers and all the thems and all the things I have done wrong.

They are stabbing me now, with knives and syringes and cutting scissors, these white-coated devils of mercy so intent on my well-being. If I could stop vomiting, if I could find my breath, I would open my mouth and tell them to end their effort, to let me find my own peace, let me become one with the rattling gears and chilled metal which make up the best of me, until the flesh sloughs away and I am distilled to a chill frost of love, and a man known and unknowing, safe from hurt, inside only the pain I have chosen, distant from mother, lover, sister, friend, drowning in only those memories I choose.

I shall swim forever in the perfect moments of my love, and where I am going, God will never find me.

The Last of the Crimes of Danni Killabrew

Danni Killabrew boards an American Airlines flight from San Francisco to Dallas. The aircraft is a 757, which should be comfortable but is not. She sits in the blue seat with the scratchy fabric and the leather headrest and stares out at the Rorschach clouds. There are faces and hands and vulvas and anuses and starfished wounds with tucked-back edges to be seen aplenty in the mighty tighty whities of the clouds, but they do not interest her.

Daddy Nekko has asked her to do a Certain Thing, and he has used a Certain Word, which means that as Danni values life, she must do it. Daddy Nekko has owned her, or at least the important parts of her, since she permanently left the fourth grade in an unmarked van driven by someone she didn't know. Every breath she had drawn, every bite she has eaten, every orgasm that has shaken her groin since that day; these things are all his property.

Even her love belongs to Daddy Nekko, though in his generous nature he allows her to job it out to promising youngsters like Markus.

In Dallas, Danni buys a pretzel from a sullen Salvadoran woman pretending to be Auntie Anne in a brightly-decorated food booth, then boards the short flight to Austin on an MD-80. That flight is just long enough for her to remember the first time Daddy Nekko asked her to do a Certain Thing. She was fifteen, and still thought she lived wrapped in love, and so she did that Thing, which bound her to him forever in chains of shared secrecy and criminal liability.

At Austin-Bergstrom International Airport she rents a comfortable car, a Lincoln with cruise control and GPS. She drives south on Highway 183, finally parking the Lincoln behind a rural cemetery. Taking only her satchel of sex toys, Danni walks to the nearest farm, where she hotwires an old Chevrolet pickup with local plates and enough mud to be noticed by no one.

From there it is a short drive to another farm where she steals certain tools from the barn. Surprising a farmhand on the way out, or possible a family son, she stabs him in the eye with an awl, then slits his tongue so he will not talk before he dies.

It is another short drive to Sail Selvage's old house with the rusting Mercury moldering in the yard and the henge of paint cans in the tomato garden. Farm tools stand in for her preferred surgical implements, but otherwise she does the Certain Thing Daddy Nekko sent her to do, with the same pride, pleasure, and professionalism that he has trained into her.

It is only later, in her second stolen car, on the way back to recover the rented Lincoln, that she stops and throws up in the bar ditch. Kneeling in the Johnson grass, gagging on death and pain for the first time in her life, Danni realizes that she actually loves Markus, himself, for her own reasons.

Her greatest crime is betrayal. Blood is business, but she has torn his heart out, though it might be that he never knows this thing.

She resolves that she will confess. Either Markus or Daddy Nekko both will likely kill her for talking.

The Lincoln has good air conditioning, and Danni is able to buy enough beer at a rural convenience store that by the time she checks in to the Quality Inn in Del Valle, Texas, just outside the airport grounds, she has all but forgotten her resolve. Thinking on the death of Sail Selvage, she masturbates long in the tub before watching old Hollywood musicals all night and never sleeping at all.

"I love you," she whispers to the gray, phosphor-lit morning, but she is no longer sure who it is that she is speaking to.

vi: Love in the Time of Flesh

When Danni finally told Markus what she'd done and why, he knew his time of love was over. He didn't understand the real why—just hers, that Daddy Nekko had asked of her something that could not be refused—but even knowing only what she told Markus, his heart road had ended.

"Thank you," he whispered to Danni. He pulled her close, the eight-inch knife that had replaced his left hand (except for the pinkie syringe) drawing tight against her neck, his right hand, intact for needle work, stroking her back. "I treasure your honesty as I treasure our love."

She began to sob, her face buried in his chest. The mesh in his ribs stung a bit, but he couldn't tell if that was post-operative pain or his own heartache expressing itself literally.

"It's okay, sweetie," he said, raising his flesh hand to smooth her hair. He began massaging the left side of her neck with his flesh hand, just behind the blood vessels, while using the flat of the blade of his metal hand on the other side.

Danni purred through her shuddering tears, but settled

further against him, relaxing into his touch. That did not seem to be a moment for cutting. He kept rubbing, relaxing and depressing her vagus nerve as her breathing slowed further until she collapsed.

Markus strapped her to his kitchen table with duct tape and some webbing hooked to bolts beneath, then rolled an IV stand into place. With long practice he set the needle in the back of her left hand, and put her on saline with a Valium drip.

He wanted Danni to still be there when he got back.

Then he packed up a collection of tools, including three fully charged tasers in case of an outbreak of map boys, and headed off to find Daddy Nekko in the name of love.

Later, much later, he came home bloody and tired. He'd left his tools behind, amid the parts and pieces of Daddy Nekko. There had been a bad moment with New York, but he'd handled it. New York and London he'd killed outright. San Francisco was somewhere out there, loose in the city he carried on his head.

Markus had every confidence that the third map boy would be coming for him soon enough.

Danni slept where he had left her, spittle pooling on one side of her lips. Her orange hair fell across her face in a loose fan, a spray of color that mirrored the bright red sprays Markus had set free in Daddy Nekko's tiled basement.

He touched her lips. They were narrow and pale, much like his mother's had been on those long-ago nights. It had been almost eighteen months since Daddy Nekko had given Markus his first implant, and she'd never followed him into the big cuts. Always an excuse, always fear. She'd pulled away from him, over and over, though she kept coming back.

And now this. The death of his mother, ordered by Daddy Nekko as one of his Certain Things, performed by his love.

Because Daddy Nekko had been jealous, had wanted Markus to learn Certain Things of his own, about safety and security and who controlled the past and who controlled the world.

"I'm your daddy now," he told his woman as she slept. Then he readied a surgical tray, readied the final melding of their love, steeling himself for what they would become together. "And we're always going to be close," he added, tracing lines upon her face with a marker.

Chamber Music of the Heart

He finally follows the flow to the source. The classical fountain of love, that clenched cliché, the human heart, his four-chambered pump driving the fatty meat of his organs and the slick, sullen machinations of his brain, oxygenating his muscles, circulating everywhere as the water of life.

The journey is swift, along the body's greatest currents, surfing the cells until he stands within the clean atrial cathedral that lies at the center of the world of his being.

"I have come for the fountain," he told the glistening muscles around him

"You are the fountain," his heart said in a voice that echoed of the four-cycle lub-dub he often heard whispering in his ears at night.

"No." Markus remembers almost everything now, even as the beat around him begins to flutter. "I am not the fountain. Love has left me."

"Love is with you forever. I am with you forever."

"There is no forever," Markus says. "Everyone dies."

"Love is still forever. It flows from you."

"And Danni . . . " He remembers so much now, almost everything, in these moments before he dies.

The heart sighs, hesitates. In some distant place, nurses shout as a doctor curses.

"Where did it go wrong?" he asks his heart.

"At the beginning."

"Was it the pain?"

"No. It went wrong with was taken from you, and never given back. You found your way through pain, but that was not enough either."

"She is with me now," he says, approaching a state of satisfaction.

"She is with you for now," corrects his heart.

There are the little matters of tissue rejection, mortality, but he carries her in his one dead eye, her green one loose in place of his brown, in the rippled skin of his abdomen where he flayed loose her face and sewed it within him, in the sliced-out tissues of her neocortex that he forced through the self-trephinated hole in the right side of his skull.

She is with him, within him, as much a part of him as all the metal and wires and cutting and pain, and he will carry her inside of him forever, far into the cold, unloving countries of the dead.

A needle plunges into the silent atrium where he stands, rupturing sac and muscle wall. Markus exerts his will, causing the fountain of love to unfold from him, blood exploding in three directions from his chest, one arm each of the abortive starfish for Sail, for Danni, and finally for himself.

"I love you," he tells the garlic-breathed nurse, staring at her through his open eye as his chest collapses in a washing sea of draining pain.

History 105

When Markus was twenty-four and dying in a San Francisco hospital of a constellation of botched self-inflicted surgeries and some truly bizarre tissue rejection issues, his sister Anna Forksmith came to visit him.

It took her two days to talk her way past the front desk and into his ward. Two days, the services of the ombudsman, and several telephone calls to the *Lockhart Post-Register* which confirmed her relationship to the almost-late Markus Selvage. And finally, the intervention of a kindly doctor.

"I don't give a fuck," Anna told a woman with a toad's face and too-tight pink nurse's uniform. "He's my brother, we just lost our mother, and I'm going to fucking see him before he fucking dies."

"Ma'am, only parents, children and spouses can—"

"He ain't got none of *them*!"

The Caldwell County Sheriff's Office was seeking a court order to take Markus into custody, surely a formality at this point, and Anna very much wanted to speak to him before he died or the cops got him. She wanted to know if he'd killed Sail, and what the hell had happened to him.

When she'd first asked for her brother, the mention of his name had caused two of the staff to head for the bathroom retching.

What the hell had *happened* to him?

No one seemed willing to say a word.

As she argued with the pink toad, a doctor came bustling in. He was a tall, irritated black man with salt-and-pepper hair and young eyes. "Are you Mr. Selvage's sister?" he asked, ignoring the nurse.

Anna knew authority when she saw it. "Yes. Are you his doctor?"

"Well . . . yes." He stared at her. "You do look like him." Then, to the pink toad: "She's with me."

"Dr. Thompson, she can't—"

"Shut up, Riley."

Anna flipped the woman the bird and followed the doctor out into the hall.

They stopped outside a locked ward. Anna was relieved to see no cops.

"Listen," said Dr. Thompson. "You look . . . uh . . . normal."

"Normal?" She was so exhausted from two days of arguing that she wasn't ready to fight about that too.

"He had a massive heart attack last night. Hemorrhaging internally from more points than I could begin to count. He has a lot of . . . uh . . . implants. Your brother was into some very strange territory, Ms. . . . . Selvage?"

"Forksmith," she corrected automatically. "But I'm Anna."

"Well. We don't know everything. Never will. I don't know why he's not dead right now. And there's something seriously wrong with his gut. He may have . . . concealed evidence . . . beneath the skin. But he's been too sick for us to go looking for it. That will have to wait for the autopsy."

91

Anna was beginning to understand why the staff had wanted to vomit at the mention of her brother's name. "So why are you taking me in now?"

"Because he's dying," said Dr. Thompson, a strange expression on his face. "Because the last few times he's said anything, he's shouted about love. Because no one should have to die alone if there's a choice."

He took out a key, unlocked the ward, and they stepped into a dim purgatory lit with the pale green and blinking red of far too many machines.

It was overly easy to say her brother looked like hell. One eye was folded, sort of, the lid almost collapsed. His cheeks were odd, squared. The rest of him was under a sheet, but the arms were . . . wrong.

And so many machines, Anna thought, *so many machines.*

"You can touch his right hand," Dr. Thompson said. "His left . . . well . . . "

She reached down, sheet between her skin and his, and stroked the side of his palm. Summer nights in the old Mercury, her and him and Tildy rolling around naked together. Not quite sex, not exactly, but close enough to ruin her if anyone had ever found out. Tildy was gone, pole-dancing in Oregon or Washington. Sail was dead now. Markus dying.

No one left but her to remember the days of their childhood innocence.

She began to giggle at that thought.

Dr. Thompson looked at her strangely as the machines beeped and squealed. One of Markus' eyes flickered open.

"She's with me," her brother said, and smiled fit to be an angel.

"Of course," said Anna, who had no idea what or who her brother was talking about.

The machines shrieked and flared, and there were nurses everywhere for a while, but Dr. Thompson never made her leave.

The next day Dr. Thompson called her. "Can you meet me at the Ground State? It's a coffee shop down on Irving."

"Sure." She'd made her plane reservations for the day after. There wasn't going to be a funeral. "Why?"

"Just be there in an hour."

She went, wondering what, if anything, she would learn about her brother's death. It was a grubby place, floors looking like they'd hosted a mud wrestling tournament, but Dr. Thompson was there without his lab coat, a ceramic cup steaming in front of him as some kind of industrial punk music blared through the speakers.

Anna felt very out of place. She was a long way from

Central Texas. But there was too much blood. She wanted an answer.

"I need to show you something," Dr. Thompson said abruptly. "I'll be fired if anyone knows I did, but you . . . you deserve to know. And maybe you can tell me what it signifies."

"Uh huh." In that moment, she did not want to know what had become of her brother, what his death might mean.

"Be warned. This will be hard. Very hard." He pushed a Polaroid photograph across the little table at her, face down. Anna picked it up, turned the picture over.

It took her a minute to understand what she was seeing. A bloody mess, red and yellow and pink and blue and black, like the scrap bucket from a butcher shop.

Then she saw the nose. Lips.

A woman's face. It was a woman's face, sewn into a larger panel of . . . skin?

"It was inside the skin of his abdomen," said Dr. Thompson gently. "Facing in and up. Toward his heart. We don't know who she is . . . was."

Anna began to cry, shaking her head, sobbing for the waste of years and lives. She collapsed onto the table, shrieking, then weeping, until finally Dr. Thompson stood, brushed his fingers across her shoulders, and left.

When she finally looked up again, a bald man was

standing at the counter, the map of a city tattooed on his head.

Only in San fucking Francisco, she thought, taking the Polaroid and preparing to leave.

The Death of Markus Selvage

The women of his life loved him, all of them, without reservation, with open hearts and open arms and open mouths, as he found his way to them through a forest of rusting blades and glittering chains and clattering gears where the sweet birds sang forgiveness in his name.

This limited edition of 1000 hardcover copies
was printed by The Maple Press Company
on 55# Maple Antique paper
for Prime Books in August 2013.